The Long White Scarf

To the memory of Private Richard Rowland Thompson, of the Royal Canadian Regiment,
who after the Boer War was the only Canadian awarded "The Queen's Scarf of Honour" for gallantry.
—M.T.

To my dear mother, Doreen Craig, who has inspired my love of history—especially
British history. As an artist she has always been there for me with encouraging
words when at times I felt like giving up.
—D.C.

Text copyright © 2005 by Maxine Trottier
Illustrations copyright © 2005 by David Craig

Published in Canada by Fitzhenry & Whiteside,
195 Allstate Parkway, Markham, Ontario L3R 4T8

Published in the United States by Fitzhenry & Whiteside,
121 Harvard Avenue, Suite 2, Allston, Massachusetts 02134

www.fitzhenry.ca   godwit@fitzhenry.ca

10 9 8 7 6 5 4 3 2 1

Library and Archives Canada Cataloguing in Publication

Trottier, Maxine
The long white scarf / Maxine Trottier ; illustrated by David Craig.

ISBN 1-55005-147-4

I. Craig, David II. Title.

PS8589.R685L65 2005   jC813'.54   C2005-903736-9

U.S. Publisher Cataloguing-in-Publication Data
(Library of Congress Standards)

Trottier, Maxine.
The long white scarf / Maxine Trottier ; illustrated by David Craig
[32] p. ; col. ill. ; cm.
Summary: A wayward scarf travels the breeze and is claimed by a series of owners
before it finds its way back, many years later, to its original home with Queen Victoria.
ISBN 1-55005-147-4
1. Scarves — Fiction. I. Craig, David. II. Title.
[E] dc22   PZ7.T 7532Lo 2005

Fitzhenry & Whiteside acknowledges with thanks the Canada Council for the Arts,
the Government of Canada through the Book Publishing Industry Development Program (BPIDP),
and the Ontario Arts Council for their support of our publishing program.

Design by Wycliffe Smith.

Printed in Singapore

The Long White Scarf

written by MAXINE TROTTIER

illustrated by DAVID CRAIG

Fitzhenry & Whiteside

The princess wore a long, white scarf. It was her special scarf, all soft and white as a silky cloud, and it had the letter V embroidered at one end. She felt very grown-up when she wore it.

That morning she wrapped the scarf around her neck before leaving the palace.

The princess rode with her mother in an open coach. A cool breeze raced along the banks of the River Thames and up the busy cobbled streets. It whirled around the coach and whipped the scarf from the princess's neck.

"Mama!" cried the princess as she grabbed for her scarf.

"Now, Victoria," said her mother with a laugh. "It is only a scarf." And she settled herself in the carriage, looking very regal. Victoria watched the scarf drift through the air and drop onto the river. It was gone.

Down the river floated the scarf as curious swallows swooped above it. Up ahead, standing knee-high in the water, a man was fishing. The river swirled and the scarf wound around the man's leg.

"What have we here?" said the man as he lifted the dripping scarf from the water. A few pale leaves clung to its surface. "This is just the thing for my Beth." His pole and creel over his shoulder, he waded out of the shallows and carried the scarf home across the meadow.

At their cottage, his wife asked, "What have you found?" Beth stood on her tiptoes to see, her little brother William clinging to her skirts.

"It is a scarf for Beth, my dear," answered her husband.

Beth's mother washed the scarf in warm water and hung it in on a line in their small garden while the children watched. The wind pulled and ruffled the scarf, but the clothes pegs held it fast. Finally, the scarf was dry.

"Here you are, Beth," said her mother, taking it from the line. Beth held the scarf to her cheek, breathing in the scent of a warm English springtime. Carefully folding it, she ran inside and placed the scarf in the small trunk in her bedroom.

For years, the scarf lay in Beth's trunk. She wore it on only the most important days. It made her feel  different, as though the white scarf alone could lift her above London's fog and dirt.

One summer, Beth stood on the side of a crowded street in London, hoping for a glimpse of the royal carriage as it carried the new queen through the city on her coronation day. The long, white scarf was wrapped around Beth's throat. Its ends waved in the breeze.

"There she is!" cried William. "There is Queen Victoria!" As the carriage rolled past, the wind mischievously pulled at Beth's scarf, but she held it tightly. She thought she saw the queen look her way, but then the carriage was gone.

Years passed by like pages in a book when the wind lifts and turns them. Then one foggy morning, the scarf covering her head, Beth went with her parents to say goodbye to William. A war had begun against Russia and William was a soldier now. Beth put her arms around her brother and held him close.

"Take this," she said, pulling the scarf from her shoulders.

"I cannot take your scarf, Beth!" cried William in surprise.

"You must," she answered, winding it around his neck. "Wear it beneath your uniform. It will surely bring you luck."

Each day Beth read the newspaper, hoping for news. Far away, William thought of home as he prepared to ride his horse into battle. The guns began to fire, filling the world with the roar of cannons and the terrified cries of horses and wounded men. When a shell landed nearby, his horse reared and William was thrown off. — Later, his captain found him crumpled in the mud.

"Carefully," he said, as a soldier loosened William's tunic. "It is his arm."

"We can use this scarf to make a sling," said another, and they carried him to the doctors.

Later, William awoke on a cot among many other wounded men. A sweet face looked down at him.

"Ah, you are awake," said the young nurse. "We have set your arm and it will mend, but you must rest." He looked around. His uniform lay folded on a chair nearby, and on it was draped the white scarf.

The nurse was named Rose. She stopped by his cot each day, and when he was stronger, she wheeled him out into the sunshine in a wicker chair and wrote letters for him. She sat with him and they talked of home.

When William was sent back to England, Rose went with him. It was a happy journey, first by land and then by sea. When England finally appeared, a pale line of land in the distance, the soldiers cheered and the nurses wiped their eyes. For them, the war was over.

"It did bring me luck," said William the day he married Rose and returned the scarf to his sister. But now, Beth thought, the scarf belonged to the whole family.

Year after year, the scarf waited in Beth's trunk, folded in the darkness. Out it would come to be arranged over the shoulders of a joyful, smiling bride or draped in honor over the coffin of a lost loved one. In time it turned a soft and delicate ivory, lacy with age.

One misty day there was a family christening. Beth carried the baby in her arms as the family walked along the river to the church. She began to tuck the scarf more closely around him, but the English breeze suddenly lifted in search of mischief. In a moment, it caught the scarf and whisked it into the air.

"No!" cried Beth, but the scarf was gone, floating into the mist like a ghost.

It fell slowly toward earth. A shopkeeper who was passing by looked up just as it caught in the low branch of a tree.

"Now, what is this?" asked the man, carefully pulling the scarf from the branch. It felt silky and soft in his hands. "This it will be perfect for the shop," he said happily.

The man arranged the scarf in the window of his curiosity shop, making certain that the letter V could be seen. He had not sat behind his counter for a moment when the doorbell jingled. An old woman and a small girl walked in.

"That scarf," said the old woman. "My grand-daughter would like to buy it."

"Of course, madame," answered the shopkeeper with a nod. "She will look very grand in it."

"Oh, it is not for me," laughed the little girl. "It is the perfect gift for someone else."

The next day the girl rode with her grandmother through the bustling streets of London. A crisp breeze blew, but the scarf had been safely placed in a box tied up with gold ribbon, and the child held it on her lap.

"Do you think she will like it, Grandmama?" asked the little girl.

"I know she will," answered the old woman. The carriage rolled down the street and turned into the open gates of a palace. When it stopped, footmen rushed to open its door. One footman helped out the queen's elderly lady-in-waiting; another held the hand of her granddaughter.

"I have something for the queen," said the child proudly, and the footman bowed.

Inside the palace, people rushed everywhere. It was the queen's Golden Jubilee, and the entire city was celebrating her fifty years upon the throne. In her chambers, the queen readied herself for the ceremonies.

"There you are," said the queen to her lady. "We thought you had forgotten us."

"Oh no, Your Majesty," said her lady as she curtsied.

"Well, child, what do you think of all of this?" Victoria asked the little girl.

"I think it is wonderful, Your Majesty," cried the child as she too curtsied. "If you please, I have brought you a present."

Victoria took the box, pulled at the gold ribbon, and lifted the lid. She picked up the scarf, fingering the letter V. She marveled at how time could work a gentle magic and, for just a while, change things. A smile creased her face.

"We will take this with us today as we ride through the city," she said.

That day, it seemed as though all of London stood in the streets with the Union Jack waving above them. Cheering and waving and singing while church bells pealed, wealthy people and poor people, soldiers and nurses—all waited for a glimpse of the queen. Some had stood there fifty years before to watch her as a young woman, newly crowned and greeting her subjects.

Inside the carriage, Victoria stroked the scarf. For some reason, on this day when she had been so weary of the weight that her rule pressed upon her, she felt strangely young. She waved to her people, the carriage rolled though the city, and Victoria's scarf rested beneath her hand.

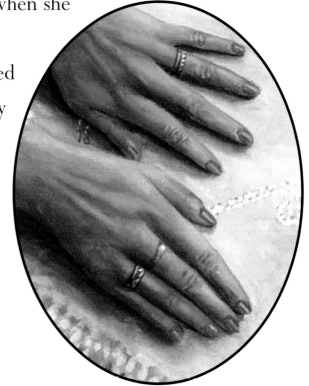

HISTORICAL NOTE

The scarf and the events surrounding it in this book are fictional. The story, however, was inspired by a unique award presented to eight courageous soldiers more than 100 years ago.

Queen Victoria sat upon the throne from 1837 until her death in 1901. Her name became associated with an entire period of English history. In spite of the fact that she was the Queen of Britain and Empress of India, Victoria was in many ways a solitary, simple person. She preferred the quiet country life at Balmoral in Scotland to the hum of London, a bonnet and a pony cart to her crown and royal carriage.

Victoria was devoted to her husband Prince Albert. Together they had a family of nine children. When Albert died in 1861, Victoria went into seclusion. She never really ceased to mourn him. It was only her Golden Jubilee in 1887 that brought her back to a public life of sorts.

In this tale, the battle in which William is wounded would have taken place during the Crimean War at the Battle of Balaclava on October 25, 1854. In 1901, when England became involved in the Boer War in South Africa, Queen Victoria crocheted eight scarves. These scarves, called "the Queen's Scarf of Honour," were presented to commonwealth soldiers who had distinguished themselves in battle. Like Queen Victoria, the longest reigning monarch in British history, they and the brave men to whom they were presented will always be remembered.